In Memory
of
Bessie Mae
Korzilius

Jackie Robinson

A Level Two Reader

By Cynthia Klingel and Robert B. Noyed

The
Child's
World®

Jackie Robinson was a great baseball player. He was also the first African American to play baseball in the major leagues.

Jackie Robinson was born in Georgia on January 31, 1919. His family moved to California when he was a baby.

Jackie as a young man →

Jackie's family was poor. His mother worked very hard for her children.

In school, Jackie liked sports. He was very good at basketball, football, baseball, and track. He quit college to help his mother earn money.

Jackie playing basketball →

Jackie was good enough to play professional sports. But black people were not allowed to play major professional sports at that time.

Jackie played baseball in the Negro Leagues. Then, he was asked to join the Brooklyn Dodgers.

Jackie signing a contract to play for the Brooklyn Dodgers →

The Dodgers was a white baseball team. Jackie played his first major league baseball game on April 15, 1947.

His first year as a Dodger was hard. Many people were unkind. Even so, Jackie played his best.

Jackie stealing home for the Dodgers →

18

Jackie won many awards as a baseball player. His team won the World Series in 1955. Jackie finally quit playing baseball in 1957.

Jackie worked hard to make things fairer for black people. He died in 1972. Everyone will remember him as one of the greatest baseball players of all time.

Jackie after being named to the Baseball Hall of Fame →

Index

To Find Out More

Books

Adler, David A. *A Picture Book of Jackie Robinson.* New York: Holiday House, 1998.

Golenbock, Peter. *Teammates.* New York: Harcourt, 1992.

Woodworth, Deborah. *Determination: The Story of Jackie Robinson.* Chanhassen, Minn.: The Child's World, 1999.

Web Sites

Jackie Robinson and Other Baseball Highlights: 1860s–1960s
http://lcweb2.loc.gov/ammem/jrhtml/jrhome.html
To see the Library of Congress's collections about Jackie Robinson.

Jackie Robinson: Breaking Barriers
http://www.majorleaguebaseball.com/u/baseball/mlbcom/jackie/jackie.htm
To read more about Jackie Robinson.

Note to Parents and Educators

Welcome to The Wonders of Reading™! These books provide text at three different levels for beginning readers to practice and strengthen their reading skills. In addition, the use of nonfiction text gives readers the valuable opportunity to *read to learn*, not just to learn to read.

These leveled readers allow children to choose books at their level of reading confidence and performance. Level One books offer beginning readers simple language, word choice, and sentence structure as well as a word list. Level Two books feature slightly more difficult vocabulary, longer sentences, and longer total text. In the back of each Level Two book are an index and a list of books and Web sites for finding out more information. Level Three books continue to extend word choice and length of text. In the back of each Level Three book are a glossary, an index, and a list of books and Web sites for further research.

State and national standards in reading and language arts emphasize using nonfiction at all levels of reading development. The Wonders of Reading™ books fill the historical void in nonfiction for primary grade readers with the additional benefit of a leveled text.

About the Authors

Cynthia Klingel has worked as a high school English teacher and an elementary teacher. She is currently the curriculum director for a Minnesota school district. Writing children's books is another way for her to continue her passion for sharing the written word with children. Cynthia is a frequent visitor to the children's section of bookstores and enjoys spending time with her many friends, family, and two daughters.

Robert Noyed started his career as a newspaper reporter. Since then, he has worked in communications and public relations for more than fourteen years for a Minnesota school district. He enjoys writing books for children and finds that it brings a different feeling of challenge and accomplishment from other writing projects. He is an avid reader who also enjoys music, theater, traveling, and spending time with his wife, son, and daughter.

Published by The Child's World®, Inc.

PO Box 326
Chanhassen, MN 55317-0326
800-599-READ
www.childsworld.com

Photo Credits
© AP/Wide World Photos: cover, 5, 9, 10, 13, 14, 17, 18
© Archive Photos: 6
© Photri, Inc.: 21
© Bettmann/CORBIS: 2

Project Coordination: Editorial Directions, Inc.
Photo Research: Alice K. Flanagan

Library of Congress Cataloging-in-Publication Data
Klingel, Cynthia Fitterer.
Jackie Robinson / by Cynthia Klingel and Robert B. Noyed.
    p. cm.
ISBN 1-56766-953-0
1. Robinson, Jackie, 1919-1972—Juvenile literature.
2. Baseball players—United States—Biography—Juvenile literature.
[1. Robinson, Jackie, 1919-1972. 2. Baseball players. 3. African Americans—Biography.]
I. Noyed, Robert B. II. Title.
GV865.R6 K55 2002
796.357'092—dc21

                    00-013170

24